CLEAN SWEEP

LARSSON SIBLING SERIES
BOOK 2

EVIE MITCHELL

THUNDER THIGHS PUBLISHING

Editors: Nicole Wilson, Evermore Editing
http://www.evermoreediting.wixsite.com/info
Illustrator: Laras Putri

ACKNOWLEDGEMENT OF COUNTRY

I acknowledge the Traditional Custodians of the lands on which I write, the Ngunnawal people, and pay my respect to elders both past and present.

I acknowledge the continued and deep spiritual relationship of the Australian Aboriginal and Torres Strait Islander peoples' to this land, and their unique cultural and spiritual relationships to the land, waters and seas and their rich contribution to society.

Always was, always will be.

CONTENT WARNING AND TERMINOLOGY

This book contains graphic and explicit descriptions of sex. The book includes references to relationship and parenting struggles, and learning to love your own skin.

The main female character does refer to herself and others as fat and chubby. She is body-positive and does so because she believes there is nothing wrong with loving the body you are in.

While all care has been taken to ensure representation is respectful and inclusive, my sensitivity readers and my personal experience is limited to our own knowledge and understanding. If there is anything in the book that raises concerns for you, please feel free to reach out to EvieMitchellAuthor@gmail.com.

CLEAN SWEEP

Erik

Nappies, poop and so many sleepless nights I was pretty sure in some countries this would be considered torture and my kids could be tried for war crimes.

Yep, I was now a dad. A dad who had no clue what he was doing. A dad who somehow ended up with two kids who weren't his but I fuc- er, I mean - gosh-darn I loved them.

Only... I needed help. A LOT of help. My house was a wreck and I needed sleep. Badly.

Enter Laura -- the Queen of Clean.

She had to be an apparition caused by my sleep-deprived mind. Cause god knew she was exactly what I'd always wanted in a woman, and one glance at her curves and pretty smile had me reconsidering the need for sleep.

Laura

Being offered my own TV show was a dream come true. As the Queen of Clean I had an opportunity to educate people about the importance of cleanliness.

Only one look at my latest project and all I could think of was dirty, sweaty, filthy things.

Erik Larsson is tempting me with sweet murmurings, beautiful babies and a helpless need for a spotless kitchen. The man knows my weaknesses... the only problem?

I'm meant to be leaving for my next assignment at the end of the month.

The Queen of Clean doesn't stick around... right?

Warning: This hilarious read involves cute babies, gorgeously helpless men, and an appreciation for a clean house that goes over oh so well. Settle in greedy reader, you might need gloves for this delicious mess.

PROLOGUE

"So, they're mine?" I watched Sheriff Tristan Rodriguez nod from across the table.

"They're yours," he confirmed, and I felt a weight lift from my chest even as another settled on my shoulders – responsibility.

"It appears that she named you on the birth certificate. Even though the paternity test proves they're not yours by blood, child services have cleared you for full adoption." He stood, holding out a hand. I grasped it, blinking as he pumped it twice, a smile breaking across his face. "Congratulations, Daddy."

"Th-thanks," I stuttered, feeling suddenly disconnected from this situation.

"Good luck," he said, clasping a hand to my shoulder and giving a squeeze.

"Umm, yeah," I muttered, sinking back down to the chair in his office as reality set in.

Shit, I'm a dad. What the fuck do I know about being a parent?

Beside me, my sons slept curled tightly around each other, their little hands clasped together. A week ago, on Christmas, these babies had been handed over to me. Their mother, a woman I vaguely remembered employing for a temporary period last year, had bequeathed them to me. I didn't know her circumstances, didn't really remember her beyond a fuzzy outline of a woman who answered our phones while my mother was on sick leave.

But she'd remembered me. Remembered me enough to give me this responsibility. Her letter said she wanted me to be the man to raise her babies. To help them grow into good men. To give them the life and love she couldn't.

"Fuck," I whispered. A hand slapped the back of my head, pitching me forward.

"Ma!"

"Language!" My mother admonished, settling into the chair beside mine and nodding at the babies. "You're not a bachelor any more, Erik. You can't be saying things like that around little ears."

God, another reason I am woefully unprepared for this responsibility.

I turned, panicked, to my mother. "Ma, I can't do this."

"Yes, you can," she corrected, leaning over and straightening the blanket covering my sons' legs. "You're just having jitters."

"No Ma, I really can't." I stood abruptly, tugging at the tie around my neck, loosening it and the top two buttons of my dress shirt. I only ever wore a suit for three reasons – business, funerals, or weddings. Apparently, I could add becoming a parent to that list.

"What do I know about kids? And two? Twins? How the fu- I mean, how am I meant to know what to do?"

"You don't. Welcome to parenthood." Ma stood, straightening to her full height, reaching out to wrap me in her arms. "Erik, you're a good man. You care, you try hard, and you'll learn. Your father, your siblings and I are all here to help you. You're not doing this alone."

I sighed, letting my mother reassure me. Call me weak, call me a pussy, I didn't care. I was a fucking momma's boy and proud of it. Hand me the shirt, cancel my man card 'cause I would die for this woman.

"You're going to be a wonderful father." She sniffled, pulling back and then dusting my jacket as if lint had somehow appeared in the last two seconds. "Now, pull yourself together and let's get these babies settled."

I sighed, rubbing a hand over my face. "Thanks, Ma."

"Congratulations, Erik." She stretched on tip toes and I bent, letting her press a kiss to my cheek. "I'm proud of you... Daddy."

I blew out a breath. "Okay," I turned, looking down at the twins still peacefully sleeping. My heart felt full, a helpless loving warmth suffusing every cell in my body. "Let's get my sons home."

CHAPTER 1

Erik

"Astrid," I juggled the phone on one shoulder, desperately bopping up and down as Leif screamed in my ear. "Please, I'm begging you. I have the buyer meeting me in less than thirty minutes. The nanny has bailed for the third day in a row, and Ma is in Capricorn Cove, wedding dress shopping with Ella." My eldest brother, Gunnar, was getting married to an amazing woman. I liked Ella, loved my brother, but today? I cursed them both. This wedding was damned inconvenient timing.

I closed my eyes as Ulf started fussing. "Please, Astrid. Please, my favorite sister. Please. I'm begging you, help."

"I'm at College," my sister told me, regret in her voice. My stomach dropped as my gaze shot to the calendar on the wall.

"Shi – I mean, shoot." I muttered registering the date. I'd forgotten to change the month... twice. "When did you start back?"

"Last week," she replied, and I heard laughter in the background. "Remember? I stayed with you for Spring Break."

I blinked then sighed as Ulf joined his brother in an effort to break the sound barrier. A familiar smell floated up to me as Leif's butt bubbled under my arm.

"Fuc- er, fudge," I muttered shifting Leif around.

"What about Liv?" Astrid asked, referring to our sister.

"She's in Grand Harbour filming." Panic clawed up my throat.

"Dad?" Astrid asked, sounding just as desperate.

"With Ma."

"Rune?" She asked, referring to our youngest brother.

Desperate times, desperate measures.

"I'll call him." I promised, praying for help. "Sorry to bother you."

"Any time. Good luck. If you need, tell Rune that you're calling in my favor."

"Favor for what?" I asked, juggling my son onto the changing table positioned in my office.

"Don't worry about it, just call it in.'"

"Will do, thanks Sis."

"Anytime."

I hung up, dropping the phone to the side and immediately focusing on my son. "Right, let's get you cleaned up then call Uncle Rune."

I pulled his onesie free, then gagged as I opened his diaper, finding a poo-ocalypse.

"God damn it, Leif. You're three months old. How is this possible? *How?*"

He gurgled at me, no longer screaming now his diaper was off. This one was my nudist. Even at three months he hated clothing. I knew he'd be ripping clothes off as soon as he gained some motor function.

I cleaned him up as best I could, attempting to keep myself as clean as possible when shit was literally getting real.

"I'm coming Ulf," I called, hearing him fussing. I finished dressing Leif, then lifted him up and set him on my shoulder. Leif gurgled happily against me, his little legs kicking as I moved to the crib and set him down, placing him beside his brother. Ulf, not one to enjoy being left alone, immediately ceased crying. He reached out, hand finding his brother. They both kicked their legs in unison, gurgling happily for a moment as they reconnected.

"You guys are lucky you're cute," I told my sons, rubbing an arm across my forehead. "It makes up for last night's lack of sleep."

I blew out a breath glancing at the clock.

"Fu- er, fudge." I muttered, reaching for my phone and dialing my brother.

"What?" He answered in his usually gruff manner.

"I need a favor."

"Nope."

"Rune, just listen. Astrid said to remind you that you owe her and that I'm calling it in on her behalf."

"Fuck," my brother muttered. "Fine, where are you?"

Relief loosened my shoulders. "Work. The kids are changed and will need a bottle in about twenty. Once done they'll sleep but—"

"Yeah, yeah. I got it," Rune hung up and I breathed a sigh.

My brother was anti-social with a capital anti, but he loved his nephews. He also owned his own business, The Literary Academy, a bookstore slash café which specialized in new and used books as well as kickass coffee and meals. He'd inherited the failing store from my grandmother when she'd finally decided to retire, and within two years had turned it into a profitable venture.

Everything taken care of (for the moment) I went to the bathroom to freshen up, catching a glimpse of myself in the mirror.

Fuck.

Dark circles rimmed under blood shot eyes. My hair looked disheveled and in need of a cut, while a thick layer of unkept scruff decorated my cheeks.

Shit. I am the living embodiment of parenthood.

The twins were sleeping more now – thank God. But they were on alternating sleep cycles – fuck you, Satan. Which meant when one was sleeping, the other seemed determined to keep me busy.

I pulled open the medicine cupboard, reaching for shaving cream, a shitty disposable razor, some eyedrops and a brush.

As I cleaned up, I praised my ma for her foresight. In addition to being my receptionist and office manager, she stocked our workshop with all sorts of useful items for times exactly like today.

Within five minutes I looked if not presentable then at least alive.

"Good enough," I muttered, tossing the razor and stowing the other items.

Back in my office, the kids were watching the mobile of little long ships, Vikings and Valkyries, and, for some reason, a dragon, dance and twinkle above their heads, their little legs kicking and arms flailing as they babbled happily.

Yep, definitely my sons.

I let them gargle away, listening with half an ear while I quickly packed a bag for Rune and mentally rehearsed my sales pitch.

This new client was a heavy hitter with cash to spend. Wanted something sleek and expensive for his wife's birthday. I'd met Nick when he'd flown me out to London just before Christmas and my life went nuclear. The guy had heard about us opening a second shop in Capricorn Cove and was prepared to sign on the dotted line – hopefully. Turns out his wife was from there – strange considering less than six months ago I'd never even heard of the place.

I wanted this sale. Bad. It'd be our first commission for the new workshop, and a great start to our expansion.

At Thor's Shipbuilding we prided ourselves on our attention to detail. Our products, be it a custom wood kayak or an extravagant fifty-foot catamaran were the finest quality available.

I had a team of twenty who worked on our projects. In addition, I had trusted contractors who I'd bring in to do custom work. This business model allowed for flexibility and financial security. If a contractor couldn't deliver to the quality I wanted, that was their issue. If the market fluctuated, I didn't have to let my core team go.

Only, these days the core team was missing two. Gunnar was in Capricorn Cove setting up our second workshop and he'd taken our foreman, Mac, with him. I was pleased our business was expanding, god knew we had more projects on the books than we'd been able to keep up with. But the loss was hitting me hard.

I'd trusted Mac to run the shop and keep shit going while Gunnar took care of the financials as well as working on the builds. I designed and built, but my role had shifted to handling clients over the last few years.

Fact was, since Dad had semi-retired, Gunnar and I had grown the business. We now sold to exclusive clientele who wanted bespoke luxury. I designed and our guys built them that dream. We'd increased our reputation and built a sustainable business that allowed us to expand even while we enjoyed the finer things in life.

Without Gunnar and Mac, much of the responsibility had fallen to me while I tried to find replacements. Yet another thing to add to my to do list, it could go right after find a new, more reliable nanny, open college funds for the boys, and pick up more formula.

"Yo," Rune greeted as he entered my office. He stomped directly to the kids, leaning down to place a hand on Ulf's stomach. "They ready?"

I picked up their bag, handing it over with a grateful, "yep."

"Cool." My brother was six foot eight and built like a brick house. He looked like a mountain, sounded like a bear, and walked with the subtlety of a pack of stampeding buffalo. Unless he was trying to be sneaky, then the fucker was quiet as a whisper. He'd scared the fucking beejebus out of me more times than I cared to admit.

"There's formula in the bag and-"

"We're good," Rune muttered, lifting Leif and putting him in the double pram. Ulf came next and I watched him settle my son with gentle hands as he started to fuss. "We'll catch you at home."

Shit.

"Can't you take them to your place?"

Rune lifted a brow, "no."

"Look, just... they've had a rough few days, and the nanny is obviously fired. Or maybe she's just run away screaming."

Can I join her?

"Anyway, I haven't had a chance to clean anything up yet."

Rune shrugged, pushing the pram through the door. "Later."

"Fudge," I muttered with a sigh knowing exactly how bad my house was. Disaster zone? Nope. More like hazardous waste dump. "Ma's gonna hear about this."

"Boss?" Ian poked his head around the door. "Guy in a fancy ass car just pulled up."

I straightened, reaching for my suit jacket and shrugging it on. "Thanks. I'm on it."

He flashed me a thumbs up then headed out.

Right. If you get through this, get the orders sorted, post an ad for a new foreman shipwright, then get the boys fed, washed and in bed, you can have a beer.

I blew out a breath, running a hand through my hair. "Let's hope this guy is worth it."

An hour and a half later I waved the client off, a signed contract in my hand and a weight off my shoulders. Ian came over, clapping a hand on my shoulder.

"He signed?"

"He signed." I confirmed. "Looks like you guys have a job for at least a few more months."

Ian grinned, his teeth standing out against the red of his beard. "Speaking of jobs, not to add to your load but your sister called."

I froze, "Astrid?"

"Nah, the harpy."

I shuddered, closing my eyes. *Liv.*

"Did she say what she wanted?"

He shook his head, saw dust puffing out from his hair at the movement. "She don't talk to the likes of me."

That's because she's got a crush on you.

I wasn't one for meddling and he'd figure it out, soon enough.

"Better call her then."

"Aye," he muttered, a little of his native Scot slipping free.

I pulled my mobile free, dialing my sister. She picked up on the first ring.

"Just listen, don't speak," Liv barked.

I braced. Experience had taught me to expect the worst when it came to Liv.

Please not an elopement. I don't want to have to bury your body.

"Rune called, your house is a pig sty. That's fine. I get it. You're a single dad, co-owner of a business, you got nanny problems. Erik, I. Get. It."

I opened my mouth to speak but she cut me off.

"But here's the deal. You can't live like that. And, I can't have my nephews living like that. So, here's what I'm gonna do for you."

I closed my eyes, pinching the bridge of my nose and sucking in a deep breath, knowing I was about to hate whatever came out of her mouth.

"My new show is taking off and we've just been renewed for a second season. The test audiences love it. *Love it*, Erik. I have a free month come Friday. Instead of taking off to Fiji like I planned, I'm gonna pack up my girl and bring her and my team to you. We'll spend the month doing our thing and get you all sorted."

Liv paused for effect. "You can thank me now."

I counted to three slowly before responding. "Liv, you know I love you –"

"Oh, I know."

"—but," I continued. "I'm fine. The boys are fine. We're *fine*. It's just been a busy week."

"Uh, no. Rune found a dead rat in their nursery."

I shot straight, "what?"

"Check family chat."

I pulled the phone away from my ear, fingers rapidly navigating to our family group chat. Sure enough, after a bunch of responses, including one from my mother threatening to immediately come home, there was the picture. A dead rat next to Mr. Snuggles.

I gagged, then bit out a curse. "Fuck."

"Yeah," Liv agreed. "Now, I have the solution."

"Tell me."

"The Queen of Clean."

I frowned. "Huh?"

"It's the show I was telling you about at Christmas, remember?"

Nope.

"Vaguely," I lied.

Liv made an annoyed sound. To be fair, Christmas day was when the twins were handed over to me – meaning everything else from that time until right this second was a bit of a blur.

"I found Laura on Instagram. She was posting a bunch of cleaning videos for her family's business. She's a fourth generation cleaner and they do everything. As in crime scenes, domestic houses, commercial, you think it, they clean it. The videos are addictive. She even made *me* want to clean."

Well that's a goddamned miracle.

My sister wasn't exactly known as a domestic goddess.

"So, I reached out and found this amazing personality on the other end. Bro, she's awesome. Like crazy pretty, hilarious, smart and never, not once, shames people for their cleaning practices. She just comes in and wants to help. It's like... if Mary Poppins and Tina Fey had a baby."

What?

"Uh-huh," I muttered, running a hand through my hair. "So, you're gonna bring her here?"

"And get your house ship-shape. You need a hand; Laura is the person to do it."

"I don't know," I muttered, thinking of the piles of dirty onesies and my never-ending laundry basket. Not to mention the dirty dishes and bottles that took up just about every surface in the kitchen...

"Erik, there was a *rat* in your house."

Shit. Time to swallow your pride man.

"Fine, when can she start?"

"Friday," Liv confirmed. "We'll arrive Thursday morning, get sorted then start filming Friday."

That gave me just two days to clean before they arrived.

"Oh, and you're staying at the parent's until Friday."

"I'm what?"

"A rat, Erik. Where there's one, there may be more. The boys could get the plague. Or have their faces eaten off in their sleep. Is that what you want, Erik? A faceless child?"

I shuddered at the image, fear and shame settling in my stomach. I needed to call Rune, get my kids outta there. "I gotta go."

"Rune's at Ma's. And don't worry, I already let everyone know I'm on it."

"Thanks," I muttered, knowing Ma would still be losing her shit.

Better add a call to ma to my to-do list.

"See you Friday, brother of mine."

"Love you."

"Love you and the boys." She hung up, leaving me to dwell in my self-pitying anger.

My boys deserve better. Fuck.

My phone rang and I looked down at the caller id.

"You're the reason I'm in this mess," I told my brother in greeting.

"A rat?" Gunnar asked. "Seriously?"

"I don't know how it got there," I groaned.

"Well, it looked pretty wet, nice and freshly dead, if that's any consolation."

"It's not."

Gunnar cleared his throat, "You know, if it's too much with the kids, and me moving here... well, Ella and I discussed it and we—"

"Stop, no." I interrupted. "Don't even go there." I ran a hand through my hair. "It's just been a rough few days. The twins had a little stomach upset, they're out of sync with their sleep cycle, the nanny is AWOL, and I was more focused on landing the Del Laurentis account than cleaning."

"Promise?"

"Swear."

There was a pause. I could feel Gunnar weighing up whether to push it. Finally, he let it go and I breathed a silent sigh of relief.

"So," he asked. "Did we get it?"

"Dude, you doubt my ability to close a deal? Of course I got it."

He chuckled, "I should have known better."

"You wound me," I said, mockingly. "For that, baby sitting duties next time you're in town. A whole weekend."

"Fine," Gunner grumbled. I heard him suck in a breath, like he was startled.

"You okay?"

"Um, nothing. I... I gotta go."

I rolled my eyes. "You saw Ella."

"Yeah."

"Is she naked?"

"New swimsuit."

I sighed. "Go. Leave me to do the work of three men while you plunder and pillage."

"Thanks, owe you."

He hung up and I looked out at the water, breathing in the salt, listening to the familiar soundtrack of my workshop.

Taking one last calming breath, I turned to the workshop, calling, "Ian? You got a minute? We need to talk rosters for this month."

The Queen of Clean better be worth it.

CHAPTER 2

Laura

The Uber pulled up to the house as I glanced at the address on my phone for the third time confirming that, yes, we were in the right place.

Wow.

The modern beach house stood at two stories with a beautiful balcony at the front, and lots of windows. Painted a gorgeous, navy blue with white highlights, the house stood amongst a cute little garden brimming with flowers, and even had a little white picket fence. I half expected a Labrador to come tearing out, tail wagging ready to greet me.

"Looks like a post card, don't it?" The driver remarked.

"Indeed," I agreed reaching for my bag. "Thanks for the drive."

"Any time, let me help you with your bags."

He got out, helping to unload my three suitcases and two boxes of cleaning products and tools from the trunk.

"You want me to bring these to the house?" he asked, pulling my hand truck free and loading it with my baggage.

Yep, I was the kind of woman who owned and travelled with her own moving equipment.

"No, thank you. I've got it from here." I smiled. "Thank you so much."

"Have a good day, Ms. Sweep."

He got in the car and pulled away while I took in the picture-perfect house once more. Gorgeous didn't even come close to the beauty of this place. It felt... serene. Peaceful. Like a sanctuary.

Like home...

I shook off the thought, gripped the handles of the truck and swung the little gate open, pushing my things along the cobbled walkway up to the porch. Wisteria vines wrapped around a small entry arbor, a beautiful, whimsical way to welcome you into the yard.

Note to self, the garden needs a weed and tidy.

As beautiful as the entry was, I couldn't

help but catalogue the few minor issues I'd already noticed. Weeds sprang from fertile soil, the flowers and bushes were beginning to become overgrown, and the grass looked a little long, as if it had needed a cut a week or two ago.

The porch itself felt abandoned, cobwebs hung from corners and I noted the layer of sand and dust that coated the porch swing. I could smell the sea and fancied I could hear the waves lapping, though I wasn't quite sure how far I was from actual water.

I raised a hand to knock on the door and heard an almighty crash follow my brisk tap. There was silence for a moment then what sounded like a male cursing. The unmistakable wailing of a baby followed.

I hesitated, wondering if I should come back.

Footsteps sounded on the other side with a deep voice calling, "Coming, Liv."

"Oh," I called. "I'm not—" the door was wrenched open as I finished saying, "—Liv." I blinked, staring at the wealth of skin before me, my mind uncharacteristically blanking.

Skin. Man. Hot. Dirty. Skin. Filthy. Man.

The chest was broad with a smattering of hair and some muscle. Not six-pack chiseled but defined enough to make me appreciate that this was someone who did manual labor.... Or went to the gym. He was covered in flour and some kind of sticky coating.

Was that... chocolate?

"Shit, you're not Liv," the person who owned the magnificent chest muttered.

I was dimly aware that he was speaking, but all I saw was a filthy dirty man.

And I wanted to ride him like a pogo stick. After I cleaned him. Preferably with my tongue.

Whoa. Down girl. Abort! Abort!

With conscious effort I pulled myself together, managing to look up and into the face of this demi-god.

"You must be The Queen of Clean," the guy said, a small smile playing at the corners of his mouth.

"Laura Sweep," I confirmed, holding out my own hand to shake. He clasped it and I about died. His hand engulfed mine, making my large one feel small and dainty. His palm was calloused but warm and strong as he gently squeezed.

I wanted that hand on me. Everywhere. Now.

Pull it together, Laura!

"Sweep?"

"Family name," I said absently. "We own

the Clean Sweep Company." My gaze dropped and I nearly swallowed my tongue.

He's wearing grey sweat pants. Please Lord, I need some help right now. Forgive me for these are not pure thoughts. Satan is tempting your girl something fierce today, Lord.

My lady parts tingled for the first time in... well, a long damn time. And I was more than happy to have stumbled across this hunk of a man.

"Come on in," he invited. "I'll just be a second. Gotta get the baby."

He turned, hurrying down the hall and disappearing. I entered, immediately assessing the situation even as I tried to shake off my attraction to my client.

The only time I ever lost control like this was when... actually. I never lost control like this. This was legitimately the first time I'd ever had my brain lock into a sexual frenzy.

Unsurprising. I mean, did you see that guy? I forcibly refocused on the house. It was... well, describing it as a disaster zone would be kind. Baby clothes, toys, books, blankets and what looked like a plate with a crusty piece of half-eaten toast decorated the entry. A quick peak into the first room showed a sitting area that had been reconfigured as a playroom. It too was a mess.

How many kids does this couple have?

Liv had been pretty vague when she'd explained this project.

"An opportunity has come up. The house is a mess and they need an urgent intervention. Can you be in Cape Hardgrave by Friday?"

I'd immediately said yes, expecting to treat this like any other job. I'd live with the family, work out their ebb and flow, try and figure out what their triggers were, and then teach them a few tips and tricks to get their house organized and improve their cleanliness.

No problem.

Only, there was a problem. A very large, very shirtless, very *attractive* problem. And my lady parts were totally on board with this particular problem.

"Sorry." The guy returned, coming back down the hall. In his arms were two babies, and I blinked as he carried them towards me looking sheepish. "Leif and Ulf are meant to be with their grandparents but I needed to grab some clothing and then there was an incident with— anyway, sorry."

I blinked, taking in the hot guy who just became even hotter as he carried the babies. "I... I need a minute," I told him, placing a hand on my chest. "What's your name?"

He frowned. "Liv didn't tell you?"

"No," I murmured, watching as one of the babies snuggled closer into the guy's chest.

"I'm Erik, Liv's brother." He hefted the babies up slightly. "And these are my sons, Leif, and this big man is Ulf."

"Well." I blinked staring at the adorable babies. "Twins. You and your wife must be busy."

"Actually, it's just me."

"Just—" I looked at the chaos with new eyes. "You're a single dad?"

"Yeah, long story but I adopted these two." He pressed a kiss to Ulf's head. "Worth every minute of crazy."

Adopted. He'd adopted twins. Be still my heart, this man deserved a blow job followed by a beer.

"Wow," was all I could manage. "You're brave."

He chuckled. "Or stupid. Verdict is still out."

His place wasn't dirty or unorganized out of neglect, it was chaos because this poor guy was living with two babies and little sleep every day on his own.

I reached across, laying a hand on Ulf's back. "Can I help you with one?"

He looked unreasonably grateful. "Actually, could you take both for a minute? I was just trying to get a load of washing on but knocked over the detergent. It's everywhere."

"Oh, why don't you look after them and I'll get it sorted?" I asked, glancing down the hall. "Which way is the laundry?"

"It's through the kitchen but—"

I didn't let him finish, immediately setting off. Cleaning was not only in my name, my blood or my job title, it was a part of me.

Some people hated cleaning. I knew that. But my earliest memories were going along with my family to jobs. Mom or Dad would hand me my own spray bottle and rag and they'd let me clean a window or dust a table. We'd listen to music and they'd press kisses to my cheeks, exclaiming over my efforts and how wonderfully spotless everything looked.

As I got older, the need to clean, to give people that *ah...* moment that came when entering a beautifully clean house, grew. When social media live videos took off, I started posting different samples showing us cleaning various filthy things. People seemed to enjoy the videos so I kept posting and people kept watching and then it got kind of crazy.

Someone had shared a video I did of cleaning dried blood off a blouse. A local news station picked it up and ran the story on their morning show. I'd been invited to discuss cleaning and they'd loved me and asked me to be part of a regular segment. Liv had seen it and contacted me about recording a series where I helped families who needed a spring clean. Next thing I knew, I had eight episodes recorded and the network wanted another season – this time twelve episodes.

Cleaning was addictive viewing, apparently. Go figure.

The kitchen was equally as filthy as the rest of the house. Food crusted across surfaces, the kitchen sink overflowing. Flour and chocolate sauce was splattered across the floor and up some cupboards.

"I knocked it over looking for the spare can of baby formula," Erik said with a laugh as we passed. "Then did the same in the laundry trying to clean my chocolate-coated shirt."

I flicked him a smile over my shoulder as I bypassed the mess. "Don't worry, I know exactly what to do to get chocolate stains out."

I found the laundry and laughed. Two giant piles of dirty washing sat on a counter. This room was just as beautiful as the rest of the house – if you overlooked the current mess.

I found the broom closet and pulled out a dustpan and brush, quickly cleaning the spilled detergent and making a mental note to add child-proof locks to my list of things to talk to

Erik about. His kids were still little but they'd be crawling soon, and a quick look in the under-sink cupboard showed a few things that could definitely hurt their little bodies.

"Thank you," Erik said from behind me as I finished cleaning the spill and began to sort the clothing.

"Don't worry about it." I offered him a grin, "I actually love cleaning."

"Well, you'd be the first in this house." He had one baby on his arm now, a bottle in hand. The other baby was on his back, expertly held there by a woven wrap.

He should have looked ridiculous, or at least a little less attractive. Instead, his hot factor increased and I found myself doing a scrupulous rub of the corners of my mouth to ensure I wasn't drooling.

"I just needed some decent clothes before tomorrow," he continued, adjusting the bottle for the little one to drink. "We're staying at the parental's while they're visiting my brother and his fiancé. This house is ready to be condemned, so I may as well go fu—um, mess up theirs."

I hid a grin as I began to sort the piles of dirty laundry. "I wouldn't go that far. It's just a little mess, nothing that can't be fixed."

"You say that now but just wait," Erik warned.

He shifted slightly, his big body brushing against the broom and knocking it over. It fell, smacking the ground and startling the babies. They both began to cry.

"Fuc—um, fudge!" He barked. He began to bop on his toes, up and down, trying to soothe the babies.

"Still having trouble self-censoring?" I asked, enjoying watching this man navigate the chaos.

He barked out a laugh. "Who knew I swore as much as I do? Never realized I had such a filthy mouth."

Oh, honey. I know exactly what you can do with that filthy mouth.

I chided myself, picking up a pile of sorted colors and placing them in the machine. I added detergent and switched it on, glancing out the external laundry door, my body immediately locking.

"What?" Erik asked, immediately coming to my side. "Is it another rat?"

"Another—no!" I laughed. "And ew. Really? A rat?"

He sighed. "It was only a little one but still...."

I shook my head. "No, it's the water."

He shifted the feeding baby and tilted his head toward the door. "You wanna see?"

I nodded eagerly.

He led me outside. The laundry sat off to the end of his house. Outside, there was a large outdoor covered entertaining area, complete with an outdoor grill, kitchen and firepit. There were some old-growth trees, a large stretch of backyard, and then a fence blocking the grass from the jetty.

"We're in the lagoon. If you take the boat down that way," he jerked his head to the left, "in about two miles you'll be in the ocean."

"Wow," I whispered watching the water gently lap. "This is incredible. Your boys are so lucky to be growing up in such an incredible house."

"Less than two months ago I lived in a little apartment over my workshop."

I raised an eyebrow. "Workshop?"

"Did Liv tell you anything about me?"

I shook my head, turning back to watch the water. "Just that you needed my help."

"Huh," he muttered. "Well, I'm co-owner with my brother, Gunnar, of Thor's Shipbuilding. We inherited the business from my dad on his retirement who inherited it from his dad and so on and so forth. We build boats. Yachts, kayaks, luxury or business, you name it we build it. We're well known, have a good client base, and have an excellent product. We're popular, and we've just expanded this year to a new workshop up in Capricorn Cove, you know it?"

"Can't say I do."

He shrugged. "Neither did I till my brother ended up there after a dodgy engine and fell into the lap of the love of his life. But the town is well-placed and we're now owners of the local marina. Expanding, and diversifying our interests. You know?"

I nodded; it was what my family had done as well. People always needed cleaners, but some were in more demand than others when the economy tanked.

"Anyways, I lived at the workshop, stockpiled my money and had a chunk of change sitting there for when I got married and wanted to settle down." He looked down at his son. "Turns out, the cart came before the horse but I'm not complaining." He sent me a rueful grin. "Wanted to buy a fixer-upper but with these two keeping me busy, Ma talked me into a move-in-ready and next thing I knew I was buying this place."

"It's perfect," I shot him a teasing grin, "if not a little messy."

He barked out a laugh. "Yeah, well it's

more work than anything else at the moment with just me. Normally Ma or my sisters help but they've been living their own lives and I'm swamped at work. It's our busy season, everyone wants to buy a boat for summer. Too bad I have to break the news that our boats take longer than a week to make."

I looked back out at the water, a contented sigh slipping free. "It may be more work now, but as they grow this is going to be a forever kind of home. Your boys will have cookouts back here, swim in the lagoon, and build a tree house, and you'll probably get a dog at some point."

"Hush your mouth," he barked, pretending to turn away from me, covering one of Leif's ears. "Don't give them ideas."

I laughed. "You've done the right thing, Erik. Your boys will thank you for it."

He made a non-committal sound in reply.

We stood outside, the sound of the water, the rustle of a slight breeze in the leaves, the smell of salt and sea, and the gurgles of babies our accompaniment.

I tilted my head to the sun, closing my eyes enjoying the warmth of the beautiful Spring day. A deliciously selfish thought crossed my mind.

I could get used to this.

A hot man, beautiful babies and a gorgeous house. Who couldn't?

Don't even go there. Ignore the pull. You know single dads are your kryptonite. Abort! Abort!

But I couldn't help the tiny kernel of... something that unfurled in me. It wasn't hope or lust or anything so simple. This was deep and earthy, grounding and solid. It felt complex and distinct.

"Can I take you to lunch?" Erik's question snapped me out of my revelry.

"Lunch?" I repeated, as if the word were foreign.

"Yeah, there's a bunch of great cafes' just down from here. Can I tempt you?"

"Of course." I watched him grin in response. For a moment his gaze dropped, brushing across my breasts and down my body. I saw the flash of approval in his eyes before he snapped back to attention.

"Let me just have a quick shower then we can go."

"Sure."

He walked away and I shamelessly ogled his ass. Tight and gorgeous. Zero regrets.

Oh yes, this man was very dangerous.

CHAPTER 3

Erik

I lay in bed that night, replaying the day's events in my head, all of which seemed to focus intensely on Laura.

Laura Sweep, a woman with curves, smiles and a wicked sense of humor. She loved kids, animals, and cleaning. She'd delighted in my house, loved our town, and jumped into helping me with the twins throughout the day.

If I had words to describe Laura, I'd say cheerfully capable. And for a single dad struggling, that was hot as fuck. The fact she was also a walking wet dream? Bonus.

God, what do I need to do to get her stay?

My cock ached. It'd been over two years since my last relationship and god knew by the time that had ended, she'd killed whatever had been left of my mojo.

Let's just say, if Dolores Umbridge had been a super-hot woman of twenty-eight, that would have been my ex.

I pushed away all thoughts of that soul-destroying woman and concentrated back on Laura. Her curves, her smile, the way she cooed to Ulf when she'd held him while I fed Leif over lunch. We'd returned and she'd helped me get the boys settled, clear out the guest room where she was temporarily staying, and then we'd sat outside watching the sunset while I'd grilled some burgers and we'd enjoyed the unusually warm Spring night.

She'd arrived a day early thanks to Liv's hapless assistant mixing up their flights.

Thank you, God.

I slipped a hand down, fisting my cock and biting back a groan as I imagined Laura walking into this room, a cotton dress swishing about her knees, a knowing grin on her face.

If she were here, I'd order her to strip, watching as her beautiful breasts bounced free. I'd get her to crawl up the bed, then drag my lips down her body, tasting and teasing until she was a rosy, flushed squirming mess of desire.

I fisted harder, knowing I was close as I

tilted my head back, imaging her taste, imagining her whimpers, hot with need for a woman I'd only met hours before.

A fractured cry stopped my desire with the power of a car crash. I swore, immediately throwing back my bed sheets and rolling to my feet as Leif's cries filtered through the baby monitor.

I hiked up my sweat pants, grimacing as I readjusted, my hard as a rock cock. It ached in protest.

I know buddy. I get it. Cockblocked. Again. Fudge.

I made my way to my kids' room, trying to think of things like poop-y diapers and baby vomit to get the monster hard-on to ease. It helped. Just.

Leif lay in his bed, his little hands clenched, his screams loud and angry.

"I know, little man, I'm here." I cooed, picking him up and pulling him to my chest. "The world is an angry and terrible place. Tell Daddy all about it."

I did the familiar parent bounce, trying to comfort my crying son as I figured out what was wrong.

Diaper is fine. Temperature feels good. He ate an hour ago so should be good. Gas?

I laid a hand on his little back, rubbing gently as he continued to protest.

"Is he okay?" A sleepy voice asked quietly from the door.

I turned, and immediately regretted looking. My hard-on roared back to life. Two-and-a-bit years of sex deprivation had regressed my libido to fourteen-year-old Erik.

Hubba hubba.

If this were a cartoon, my eyes would have bulged out of my head, my tongue rolling right to the floor.

Laura was stunning.

She wore tiny sleep pants and a long shirt. Her breasts were free under the material and I could just see the outline of her nipples.

Jesus man, you're a father now. Get your mind out of the gutter.

But I couldn't. I really, really fucking couldn't. I wanted to kiss up her curvy legs, wanted to fuck those tits and cum all over her body. I wanted to taste between her legs until she shattered then do it all over again.

I must have given myself away as awareness spiked in the room. Her gorgeous nipples hardened under my gaze, a delicious blush coloring her cheeks.

"D-did you want a hand?" she asked,

crossing both arms over her ample chest and blocking my view.

Yes please.

I mentally chastised myself for the barrage of mental images of exactly where I wanted Laura's hand to go.

"I think we're good," I said, regretfully. "Thanks, though."

Just as I said it, Murphy's Law kicked in and Ulf began to stir breaking the tension.

"Shi—shoot." I sighed. "Actually, would love a hand. Can you take Ulf? He normally only wants a cuddle."

"Naww." Laura walked over to the crib, lifting Ulf and pulling him close. "Are you a little snuggler?" she asked, settling in the rocking chair beside his crib.

I continued to pace, knowing Leif would eventually settle. His hiccupped cries already starting to slow.

"For some reason you expect twins to be the same. Same looks, the same little mannerisms. And this young, you don't expect them to have personalities. Like, they're too little to be anything but a sleepy little ball of cuteness. But that's really not the case. Leif is my loud kid. Always wailing his desires, letting the world know he's here and he wants everything now.

Ulf is quieter. He loves to cuddle, will just relax in your arms and let you hold him without protest for hours." I smiled down at my boy. "Can't wait for them to start talking."

Laura's chuckle was soft and pleasing, my dick jerking his approval.

"Be careful what you wish for," she said, pushing off with one foot and setting the chair to a gentle rock. "My sister's kids are nuts. From the time Arabella could speak she hasn't shut up. And she's sassy. I babysat her and her brother a few months back. Her brother had a fall while I wasn't watching and she immediately told me she wouldn't nark if I gave them candy." She chuckled again. "Little scammer."

I found myself smiling, the bone-aching tiredness I'd lived with for months briefly fading. "I expect life will be crazy, but I'm looking forward to it."

Laura bit her lip, tilting her head to one side as she considered me.

"You want to know why I took them on."

She huffed out a laugh. "That obvious?"

"Nah, it's just the same question everyone asks."

I pulled Leif closer, breathing in his baby smell. His little hand reached out, brushing the side of my face as he watched me with big, sleepy eyes.

"When they were handed to me my first thought was no fuc—I mean, fudging, way I could do this."

Laura dipped her head, but not before I caught a glimpse of her amused smile.

"But then, I don't know. I read the note their momma left me, and I saw their tiny bodies. It had snowed, and I remember thinking, how can I toss them out into the cold?"

I shook my head, shooting her a grin. "They wouldn't have been in the *actual* cold. The Sheriff was there, and I'm sure they would have called Child Services or something." I looked back down at Leif. "But it was Christmas. And they were screaming and there were no toys for them and I just thought, wow. I need to do something."

"And you did."

I nodded, looking back at Laura. Her eyes were warm with approval, her face tinged with a little pink. In her arms, she held my son, his sweet little body turned into her.

"Yeah, best decision of my life," I admitted, shifting Leif slightly. "Hardest too. And loudest. And messiest. But the best."

"Well." Laura stood, taking Ulf over to his

crib and gently lay him down. "I can't help with the loud, but I can definitely help with the messy."

Can you help with the hard too? My cock asked.

Fuck, I'm a bastard.

She grinned at me, a sparkle in her eye. "I spoke to Liv tonight, she told me the name of the episode."

I braced.

"D.I.L.C. Daddy I'd like to Clean." She chuckled as I sighed, rolling my eyes.

"Liv is a nut."

"I love her," Laura declared, coming to me and holding her hands out for Leif. I let him go and she took him to the rocking chair, settling back down. "She's making my dreams come true."

"You dreamed of being a reality TV star?" I asked, eyebrows rising in surprise.

"Nah." She set the chair to rocking, tucking Leif's body close to her. My squirmy kid immediately settled, blinking up at her in surprise.

Oh, so you'll do it for her but not for me. Traitor.

Not that I blamed him. I wouldn't mind being snuggled up to those breasts right now either.

Down, boy.

"My real dream is to branch out on my own. My family all have their place at the company. But I was an unexpected surprise. Baby number five. The odd, very late, addition. No one really knew what to do with me, and I needed to find my own place." She shrugged. "Turns out, this is what I'm good at. Helping people."

"Does it stick?" I asked, watching her with an almost trance-like obsession.

"Does what stick?"

"The cleaning tips. The families you help?"

"Oh." She chuckled. "Sometimes, yes. I have a private group where they all send me questions and share cleaning hacks. One family immediately reverted back to their former ways – but they had bigger issues than I could help with. But others take it on. They just never got taught how to do things or thought that cleaning products were too expensive or a million other myths."

"Do you enjoy it?"

"Love it," she said, flashing me a smile. "There's nothing more satisfying than helping people. And a clean environment, an organized environment, it helps people be creative, and restore balance. It gives them the space to reconnect. Your environment is so—"

she cut herself off with a laugh. "I'm preaching, sorry."

"It's fine." I tried unsuccessfully to hide a yawn. "I'm seriously interested but it's late and I've barely scrapped together three hours of sleep over the last two days."

"Go." Laura lifted a hand making a shooing movement. "I've got these two. Go sleep."

I blinked. "I couldn't do that."

But god is it tempting.

"Sure, you can. I have stellar babysitting references, a great smile and know how to change a diaper." She jerked her head at the door. "Go. If I need anything, I'll call you."

My feet led the way, the temptation of sleep too much. "If you're sure...?"

"Insist." She laughed. "I've got this."

I went back to bed, faceplanting on the mattress and letting out a long, satisfied sigh.

"He's a good daddy," I heard Laura murmur through the baby monitor. "You're very lucky to have him."

Leif gurgled and she laughed quietly. "Oh yes, you are. So, so lucky, aren't you?"

I smiled, eyes closed, listening to Laura's calming voice and my kid's soft sounds as I drifted off to sleep.

CHAPTER 4

Erik

Whose idea was this?

I silently berated myself as my sister, my own flesh and blood, gleefully led a camera team around my house, pointing in horror at new hygiene issues to film.

"I found mold!" Someone yelled excitedly from my downstairs bathroom.

"I've got dust," another called from the lounge room. "Layers of it."

A grown man shouldn't sound that excited by dust.

Laura stood in my kitchen, her hair and make-up being touched up as we waited for Liv to get her shots.

This was day two of what I assumed would

be a never-ending filming cycle. Yesterday hadn't been this bad.

I'd woken from the best sleep I'd had in months to find Laura had fed, changed and moved the twins downstairs, Mozart playing as she'd dangled soft toys for them to grab. She'd made me breakfast, smiled at my sleepy questioning, then directed me to shower.

I'd planned on taking her and the boys out for a quick walk but Liv had arrived, entourage in tow. We'd spent the day doing posed pictures and filming shots of me with the boys. Laura had explored the house while I'd been otherwise occupied.

I gritted my teeth, going in search of my sister.

"Liv," I called, tracking her down in the twins' room. "We need to talk."

She made a dismissive gesture, directing the cameraman to film something in the boys' toy chest. Of all the rooms in the house, this one was the cleanest. I made sure of that.

"Liv," I barked, finally losing my patience. "Now!"

She sighed, straightening and moving to me. "Didn't figure you for a diva."

"Liv." I sucked in a breath, forcing calm into my tone. "Here's the thing. You can't do anything that could put me at risk of losing the boys, or bring my business into disrepute."

She frowned. "Why on earth would you assume I'd allow that to happen?"

I blew out a breath, crossing my arms over my chest. "This is overwhelming, Liv. I legitimately don't know if I should be grateful or shitting myself. There are people everywhere, you hired someone to nanny my kids, there's a woman currently picking through my junk drawer." I shook my head. "Everyone has dirty laundry, mine's now gonna be on TV."

"Yeah," Liv replied, getting close and laying a hand on my arm. "But only in a way that makes it seem like you're overwhelmed."

Which I am.

"Which you are," she said, giving my arm a slight squeeze. "And that's okay. The narrative we're pushing is great dad, loves his kids, successful businessman, just overwhelmed by the sudden changes in his life and needs a little help." She smiled. "I've got this, bro. You're safe. The boys are safe. I'm not going to do anything to jeopardize your life."

I let out the breath I'd been unwittingly holding. "Right, of course. Thanks."

Liv chuckled. "You've got nerves. You're

fine, Erik. Just breathe. We're all only here to help."

I nodded, still not entirely convinced but willing to try.

"Great, gotta get back to it. Go find Laura in the kitchen, she'll fill you in on her first suggested change and we'll get that filmed in an hour once the kids go down."

With that, Liv turned back, directing the camera guy to take a sweeping shot of the room.

Dismissed and only slightly less anxious, I left, heading for the kitchen.

Laura stood at my island bench, a clear laundry tub filled with soapy water on one side, and a pile of dirty bottles on the other.

"You ready?"

I came around, standing beside her. The production crew shuffled about, everyone getting into place.

"I mean...." I nodded at the crowd avidly watching us. "Sure?"

She chuckled. "Just concentrate on me. It gets easier, promise."

Oh, baby. I'll concentrate on you every day.

I shoved the thought aside, subtly shifting. Turns out Laura was a magnet for my dick.

"Okay," Liv called, settling in beside the camera guy. "Let's get this started." She looked at us. "Quiet guys, and action!"

Laura smiled straight at the camera. "If you're not a parent who breastfeeds, then today we're going to be talking about one of the most important cleaning actions a parent can do in the kitchen when they have young ones—sterilizing bottles."

She proceeded to explain the importance of good sterilization and the reason behind it – stopping bacteria. I listened, interested and at the same time a little aroused by how good she was at this. Laura... sparkled. She gave off this energy and warmth that said, *I'm not here to preach, I'm here to help*.

And I lapped it up. I watched her dip the bottle into the soapy water, explaining where people should pay particular attention when cleaning.

"These days, most bottles are dishwasher safe, but it's worth us knowing what to look for when we pull them out. Dishwashers do a great job and save a lot of time, but they're not perfect." She then turned to me. "Erik, can you assist?"

The cameras and lights followed me as I dipped my hands into the hot water and followed her instructions.

"Very good," she praised, holding up my cleaned nipple and bottle. "Now, we're going to talk about how to store this in an easy-to-organize way. As Erik knows, the worst thing is trying to find a bottle and lid during early morning feedings, am I right?"

I chuckled. "Try telling a three-month-old to wait for his food. You wanna know what hell looks like? My kid can definitely tell you."

We both laughed.

"Cut!" Liv yelled, immediately coming to stand beside us. "That was amazing, you guys. You're absolutely sparking together. The chemistry is," she raised a fist to her lips, pretending to blow on a burn. "Sizzling."

I rolled my eyes. "Thanks, I think."

"We're resetting for the pantry so that gives you five. Grab a drink or whatever and we'll get set up." Liv strolled away, disappearing back into the chaos.

"Gonna admit, never thought I'd find learning how to clean interesting."

Laura laughed. "No one ever does."

"Do you want to have dinner with me?" The words flowed out of my mouth before I could rethink the proposition.

Laura froze, her mouth forming a small 'o'. "Really?"

"Shit, sorry." I ran a hand through my hair. "Fuck, that was bad right? Sorry."

"No, I mean," she cleared her throat. "I'd love to."

I perked up. "Serious?"

"Yeah." A warm grin split her lips. "Seriously."

Yes. Don't you fuck this up.

I cleared my throat. "Great, I'll organize a sitter. Next weekend work?"

"Sounds perfect."

We grinned at each other for a protracted moment.

"Laura, can you come here a minute?" My sister called from the living room, breaking the awareness between us.

"No rest for the wicked." Laura sighed, rolling her eyes good-naturedly.

I watched her move through the room, unashamedly watching her ass, my cock throbbing his approval.

You're not fourteen anymore, dickhead. Pull it together.

I did, but god it was hard.

CHAPTER 5

Laura

"Erik," I said, exasperated with the man. "What on earth are you doing?" He looked up from where he was seated in his massive garage, piles of junk haphazardly scattered around him.

"Sorting." He lifted a yearbook he was currently perusing. "Gotta check if it sparks joy, right?"

I sucked in a calming breath and then slowly blew it out, incredibly aware of the cameras capturing every moment. "I left you here three hours ago. Three hours. What have you done during that time?"

He gestured to a shoebox. "Figured what I want to get rid of."

I heard a strangled laugh from the crew behind me.

Calm, Laura. Stay calm.

Erik, it turns out, may have moved from a tiny apartment to this giant house, but it hadn't stopped him from hoarding things in a storage container. A very large, very expensive storage container.

I'd never seen Liv more excited than when we'd cracked that baby open and a box had immediately tumbled out, spilling its contents on the concrete entry. The contents being, wait for it, empty used tissue boxes.

I still twitched thinking about it.

"Magnificent television," Liv had declared, practically dancing with delight. "My brother is a hoarder!"

Erik had protested, but even I had to admit he seemed to have difficulty letting things go. I mean, used tissue boxes?

Erik had explained that he used the cardboard when creating lettering for different painting projects. But I wasn't so sure.

It had taken a full day but we'd cleared all the junk and brought it back to his house, unloading it in his garage.

I tasked him with getting down to the bare minimum. In three hours, he'd only managed a shoebox. A freaking shoebox?

Breathe Laura. Even perfect men have their issues.

I crouched in the garage, reaching for the box and rummaging inside. There were three receipts, a stray button, two bent paper clips and a chocolate wrapper inside.

"Erik," I said slowly, clearly articulating each word. "Please don't tell me this is it."

He tilted his head to the side, giving me an eyebrow lift. "Are you disappointed?"

Calm!

"I'm not disappointed, just... surprised," I said finally. "There's a lot still to get through if this is it."

"It took me a while to double-check check the button wasn't from one of my existing shirts."

I blinked once. Then again. My vision clouding with grey as Erik watched me. For a beat he looked utterly genuine then his lip twitched, his eyes brightening right before he burst out laughing, slapping a hand on his knee.

Behind me, I heard the crew laugh.

"You goddamned liar." I snatched a stuffed animal and threw it at him. "You're already done!"

He caught it easily.

"Mostly," he agreed, still chuckling. He tossed the toy from hand to hand. "Gotcha."

"Totally." I reached for the yearbook. "Now show me your photo."

Erik groaned, then flicked through presenting me with an image I wasn't expecting.

"Glasses and braces," I laughed, delighted by the unexpected sight. "You were head of the drama club?"

"Four years," he agreed. "Never did land an actual role. Turns out I'm not very good. But I was enthusiastic."

I patted him on the shoulder. "I'm sure that counted in your favour."

He laughed. "Not even once."

I looked around at the space. "So, getting back to this mess. What can go?"

Erik gestured at a pile of furniture and boxes. "That's for the house." He twisted, nodding at another rough pile. "That's for donations, and that," he pointed to the last rough pile. "Is junk and can be tossed."

I eyed the second-largest pile. "And exactly where in your house are these things going?"

Erik hesitated.

"You were going to say the attic, weren't you?"

He huffed out a laugh, shrugging. "They're things the boys will use when they get older."

I pushed up, crossing to the pile and

beginning to sort through it. "Okay, the desk can go in your office – you need one. This." I held up a ratty jersey. "You really want to keep this?"

"Hey." Erik snatched it away from me, hugging it to his chest. "This is a prized possession."

I quirked an eyebrow, sceptical.

"This, my friend, is a St Johanna Eagles jersey. A jersey that I wore every single day of the 2018-19 season. The season, Laura, where they started as the lowest team in the entire competition. Fifty-four years without a Championship win. Everyone gave them zero chance of a change. They lost a coach before the season, and had a rookie goalie. No one but the fans believed in them. Then they won eleven games in a row. They made it to the Northern Island Conference finals. Then the Championship finals. Then they won the whole thing. The whole damned thing, Laura." He lifted the jersey. "It took me all season but I got every single signature." He gave me a serious look. "And I didn't even touch on the babies, puppy or Allison and Bob."

Bob?

"The Northern Island Conference?" I asked. "You don't live anywhere near there."

"But my ma is born and raised, and my grandparent's bleed blue all year long."

"Well, hand it over then." I gestured at him. He hesitated then gave me the jersey, watching suspiciously as I smoothed it out then held it up to the light, examining the fabric and noting the placement of the signatures.

"What are you going to do with it?" He asked, watching me like a hawk.

"You'll see." I tossed it over my shoulder, gesturing towards the internal door. "Now, would you like to see your newly improved kitchen?"

"Lead on."

The crew followed us; a second crew was already set up to capture Erik's reaction. He didn't disappoint.

His mouth dropped open, his eyes bugging out of his head as he looked around. "I have white tiles."

I laughed, nodding. "Yeah, turns out they just had years of grime build up. A deep scrub and soak and that backsplash looks like new."

"Damn," he muttered, running a hand over the kitchen benchtop. "I haven't seen this since before I moved in."

He wasn't wrong. The kitchen had been particularly heinous.

I opened his pantry, gesturing for him to come see.

"Holy... wow." He remarked, surprised at the orderliness. "I can actually see what I own."

"I know!" I chirped, incredibly pleased by his reaction. "I even bought you a labeller so you can create your own containers in future."

"Did you organize the contents of my fridge too?" he asked, looking a little shell-shocked.

"Actually..."

Erik laughed, moving to the fridge, opening it, then laughing again. "You did."

I shrugged. "Got to do a thorough clean."

I guided him through the kitchen, explaining how we'd change a few cupboards to drawers, and showing him how to use the new kid safety locks we'd placed on them. I showed him where I'd stored his various items, and guided him through the new process I'd put in place to make his life easier by food prepping.

"Seriously, Laura. I can't thank you enough." Erik said, looking overwhelmed. "It may not seem like a lot to you, or to others. I mean, it's just some drawers and some cleaning. But this is gonna save me. I haven't had time to do anything but eat, sleep, feed babies and work since the twins came. And even the sleep

is in pretty short supply." He quirked a smile
my way. "Seriously, thank you. This is huge, I
feel like a weight has been lifted off me."

"You're welcome." I finally said, emotion
welling up. "Now, should we get started on
your living room?"

He laughed, "no rest for the wicked?"

"No rest when there's mess," I corrected
with a cheeky smile.

"Then lead on, Queen of Clean."

"And cut," Liv called. I snapped back to,
suddenly reminded of the camera crew.

"That was great guys, let's reposition in the
living room. You've got five for a break while
we get sorted."

Erik reached out, capturing my hand before
I could walk away. "Queenie, seriously. Thank
you."

I made a dismissive gesture with my hand.
"Anyone can do this."

"But you did it for me. And for my boys.
And that means something."

I tried to reply but found myself at a loss for
words. Erik's expression was deadly serious, his
gratitude palpable.

"Any time," I finally said.

He squeezed my hand and then let it go.
"Guess we're in the living room?"

"Uh, yeah." I replied. "Just give me a minute."

I made my way to the bathroom, splashing a little water on my flushed face.

Damn, that man is trouble.

And yet, I didn't want to stay away.

Silly girl.

CHAPTER 6

Laura

On Friday, after a little over a week of constant filming, the camera guys stood down, leaving Erik and I with an empty house for the weekend.

"Pizza tonight?" he asked, shutting the door on the last crew member.

"Perfect," I replied, reaching down to scoop up a rag someone had left behind.

Erik's house was slowly coming together. We'd cleaned the kitchen from top to bottom, reorganized his cabinets, and worked at streamlining his functionality in the kitchen. He'd already seen the benefit after a fairly hectic night with the twins, who'd both picked up a mild bug.

"God." He scrubbed a hand over his face. "I'm wrecked."

"Why don't you have a—" my suggestion was broken by the screaming of a baby. Erik sighed, straightening and moving to the stairs.

"Coming buddy," he yelled, taking them two at a time.

I hesitated, there was only Ulf's cry this time and I decided not to go up and offer assistance. Instead, I went to the laundry room and took care of the piles of clothing, making a mental note to focus here next.

Many didn't know it, but a well-organized laundry could save people hours out of their week. Also, pro-tip, buy wrinkle-free clothing. Unless you were going to a business interview or needed to wear a suit week-on-week, investing in wrinkle-free clothing freed you from a life of ironing.

Best. Tip. Ever.

I transferred the first load to the dryer and set the next lot to clean. Ordinarily, I liked to line dry, but with two babies in the house, clothing was a constant need.

I picked up a folded load and went to the twins' room, finding it empty. I put away their tiny clothes and then went in search of Erik and the boys.

I found them in Erik's room.

I'm gonna have to clean the bedroom cause I'm pretty sure my ovaries just exploded.

Erik was passed out on the bed, the twins nuzzled into either side of him, all of them sleeping peacefully.

DILF. The man is a DILF. I am in sooo much trouble.

I stood there, just taking in the quiet peace of this beautiful man and his two sons. I couldn't deny the chemistry between us. Liv, the crew, and even the nanny had commented on it. We revolved around each other, joking and laughing to such an extent Liv had asked if we wanted to co-host a show.

Erik had declined, but I couldn't help but wish he'd said yes.

And that's terrifying.

My life was in Grand Harbour. My family lived there; my core business was there.

But you could work from anywhere...

I shook off the tempting thought. My career was just beginning, my world expanding in a way that I'd never imagined.

Not to mention you've only just met the guy and he has two other pretty big priorities. Hell, you haven't even kissed him yet.

Yeah, I really needed to get my head on straight and my mojo locked down. Travelling for a potential four months of the year wasn't exactly conducive to a stable family life.

On silent feet, I backed out of the room, leaving the sleeping boys and their incredibly yummy daddy to their nap. I headed back to the laundry but startled as I entered the kitchen, finding Liv seated at the island.

"Jesus." I pressed a hand to my thundering heart. "Warn a girl next time."

Liv chuckled, holding up an open bottle of white wine, eyebrow raised in question.

"Please," I said as I passed her. "Let me just get this last load of washing on and I'll be right back."

I swapped out the wet clothes with dirty ones, setting to the spin cycle and loading the dryer before returning.

Liv held her glass in one hand, twirling it absently, her head cradled in the palm of her other hand.

"You okay?" I asked, sliding onto the stool beside her and reaching for my glass.

"Mm," she murmured, her eyes glued to the wine.

I let her have silence, both of us decompressing after a long week.

"You know, I'm conflicted," Liv finally said, breaking the companionable silence. "I have this friend, she's talented, a hard worker, hilarious, and oh so wonderful. She's also the host of my most popular show." She tossed me a grin but it faded a moment later, her eyes locked with mine. "And she's the first woman my beautiful, generous, loving brother has shown interest in for years. She sparkles when he speaks to her, he lights up when she enters the room."

Liv paused, considering me.

I swallowed past the lump in my throat. "And your dilemma?"

"Do I encourage this because I know these two people would be perfect together, or do I discourage them knowing it's just as likely there will be heartbreak?"

I opened my mouth, words failing me.

"Hey, anyone home?" the question came from the entry, the sound of a door slamming followed the voice. Upstairs, I heard a piercing cry, the noise waking the babies.

Liv sighed, her lip pressing into a thin line. "Drink your wine, Laura. We're gonna need it."

"Sorry!" the voice called cheerfully from the entry. I heard the sound of boots clopping down the hall then a head poked around the kitchen doorway.

Furry. Red. Sasquatch.

The yeti-come-man was the furriest person I'd ever seen.

"Ah, I see the harpy is here," the man-beast said with glee, pulling off his cap and slapping it against his thigh. Dust poofed out at the action, gently floating to the floor.

My eye twitched but I ignored the compulsion to get a dustpan and brush.

"You must be Laura." The man bounded over his actions like that of an oversized baby bear. "I'm Ian." His paw of a hand swallowed mine as he shook it enthusiastically.

Unlike his cap, the rest of him was clean.

"Nice to meet you," I said politely, shifting in my seat to make a move. "You want a beer?"

"Don't fash yourself, I've got it." He walked to the cupboard, removed a glass then reached for the wine. I saw Liv's eyebrows rise before she wiped her face clear. I ducked my head, hiding a smile.

Ian took a sip and then grinned, "I see you bought the good stuff. Nice taste."

I nodded at Liv. "Actually, Liv bought it."

He considered her with renewed interest over the rim of his glass, swirling it gently.

She ignored him, purposefully looking at me. "So, what are we doing for dinner?"

"Pizza," Erik said, entering the kitchen, a baby on each arm. "Already ordered. And yes —" he said before Ian or Liv could comment. "—I ordered no pineapple."

They glanced at each other, then immediately looked away, both taking a long drink of their wine.

"You want me to take one?" I asked Erik, holding out my arms for one of the babies. He handed me Leif then went to the fridge, snagging a beer. "Thanks for letting me sleep." He rubbed an arm over his face. "God, I needed that."

I grinned, then looked down at Leif who pulled at my top, his hand firmly fixed. "Did you have a good sleep, little man? Hmm?"

He blinked up at me, giving me a big smile.

"Such a handsome boy," I cooed swaying around the kitchen. "You want some dinner?"

Ian moved, placing his glass on the island and pulling the cupboard open, calling, "I'll get you some yummies. Let's see." He pulled a tin of formula, holding it up triumphantly. "Gourmet baby milk? Delicious!"

He danced around the kitchen, surprisingly agile for a man of his size, humming *Be our guest* from Beauty and the Beast. Liv appeared unable to process Ian's antics, instead pouring her an overly generous second glass.

After the babies were fed, we settled them in the lounge room, soft toys on their chests to distract them while we all devoured the pizza.

The evening was enlightening. I learnt that

Erik was an absolute sweetheart to everyone in his broader orbit – as evidenced by his and Ian's close relationship. Liv dropped the occasional embarrassing story, and he constantly checked in on his boys.

Apart from being a bit of a mess, the guy is near perfect.

"I got this," Liv muttered, getting off the sofa and clearing the remains of our dinner. "Besides, I better hit the road."

"Big weekend?" I asked, perfectly content to continue tickling Ulf's feet, his chubby legs kicking out at me as he gurgled his delight.

"Something like that," she muttered.

"I better be getting on too," Ian said, stretching. "Your pa asked me to help get the duplex sorted for the new apprentice."

"This is the girl Gunnar recommended?" Erik asked from his position beside me on the floor. He was holding a set of dangling soft scarves for Leif to grab.

"Yeah, gotta install the extra safeties tomorrow for her."

"You need a hand?"

"Nah, mate. Rune's gonna help but we should be good. Thanks," he leaned down, jiggling each baby's leg gently. "Farewell boy-o's. You be good for your daddy-o."

He stood, throwing me a smile. "Night, Laura. Thanks for helping out our main man."

"Any time," I said, pushing to my feet.

We waved Liv and Ian off, both of them bickering as they walked down the path to their cars.

"Not sure how I feel about that," Erik muttered, watching them from the window in the sitting room.

"That they're attracted to each other?"

"Mm." He shook his head. "Wish they'd just sleep together and get it over with. I'm sick of the bickering."

I chuckled, watching Leif start to yawn. "Your sister is great, except for the fact she's the most sexually repressed woman I've ever met."

Erik made a gagging sound. "TMI, woman!"

I rolled my eyes. "Why do brothers have such an issue with talking about sex?"

"Uh-huh, nope. The only person's sex life I'm interested in is yours."

We both froze.

"I meant mine, sorry, mine," Erik corrected in a hurry, swearing under his breath. "Fuck, I mean, fuck, fudge, fu—ah, hell." He shut up.

I tilted my head to one side, "Erik, have you been thinking about what sleeping with me would be like?" I tried not to grin as I teased the poor man.

"Fuck it," Erik muttered. He threw back his shoulders, looking me straight in the eye. "Yeah, I have. How do you feel about that?"

Instead of answering I closed the distance between us, raised up on my tip-toe and kissed him. He allowed it for a beat, then took over.

Holy shitstacks. Who the fuck let this guy kiss? He needs to come with a warning label.

Erik didn't kiss, he devoured. He let my lips caress his for only a moment before he took over, plundering my mouth in a way that felt oh-so good.

His hands came to my waist, pulling me closer, one hand stayed there while the other trailed up my back, fisting into the hair at the back of my neck.

Holy shit. Ho-ly sheeeeeeeiiiit.

The words rolled around in my head on repeat as he kissed me, over and over and over again. His mouth trailed from my lips dipping to taste my neck.

"Delicious," he muttered against me, his teeth grazing against the sensitive skin. "So soft."

I pushed his mouth to my skin, groaning when he took the hint and began kissing and sucking. He felt amazing, my body coming alive under his hands, his mouth, his tongue.

Erik backed me to the couch and I dropped onto it, my legs finally giving out. He followed, dropping to his knees before me.

"Need to taste you," he grunted, his hands falling to my pants. "Get these off."

Together we pushed and pulled them down my legs, my underwear coming along for the ride. He fell on my pussy, his lips tasting and teasing, his tongue stroking. There was no other word for it, the man *worshipped* me.

A gurgled sound had us both freezing. Our heads whipped to the floor where Ulf and Leif were both sleepily settled on their little mat.

"Crap," Erik whispered. "Do you think they saw?"

A hysterical giggle burst from my lips. "I don't know. How far can a three-month-old see?"

"God, I'm gonna have to take them to therapy."

I lost it, my head tipping back as I roared with laughter. It took Erik a beat but he joined me, his head resting on the inside of my thigh.

As we calmed, I found that I couldn't stop stroking my fingers through his hair.

"Guess we better call it a night," Erik sighed.

"Yeah," I agreed, the needy desire dissipating. Amusement and an aching sense of missed opportunity filled the void. "But just FYI, you can go down on me anytime."

Erik winked, rising to his feet and hauling me off the couch. "Let me put the boys down then Netflix and actual chill?"

I blew out an exaggerated sigh. "Fine. I'll take your scraps."

Erik pulled me into his side, dropping a kiss on my head as he laughed.

"Queenie, my scraps are worthy of a gourmet meal."

"Promises, promises."

CHAPTER 7

Erik

"I get it, I owe you." I handed over Ulf to Rune. "I'll be back tomorrow. There's formula and bottles in the cooler bag, their blankets in the –"

"I got it," Rune rumbled, lifting Ulf a little higher. "Go."

I hesitated. My brother had looked after my boys a few times but it didn't make leaving them any easier. I suspected it would be like this no matter their ages, be they three months or thirty years.

Rune shut the door in my face, and I sighed. My brother, for all his gruffness loved our family, and particularly his nephews, fiercely. I just wished he'd find a partner and settle down; god knew a little time between the sheets might improve his attitude a little.

Speaking of...

I made my way back to the car; Laura was on her phone with her agent. Something about an endorsement deal for an environmentally friendly product she loved.

She saw me, flashing a bright smile and a wave as she continued to chat on the phone. I slid in the driver's side, setting us off as she wrapped up her call.

"Thanks, Merry. Yeah, I'll have a read over the terms but if you think it's good then I'm sure it is." She paused then laughed. "No, but thanks for the vote of confidence. I'll chat to you later. Bye."

She hung up, dropping the phone in her clutch. "Sorry about that. Turns out this was a bigger offer than we were expecting, and Merry wanted to chat through the changes."

"Endorsement deal, right?"

"Yeah. It'll be my first major sponsorship. But part of the terms is that they give a percentage of sales for a particular product to a clean water charity."

"Clean water charity?"

"Oh gosh, yes." Laura nodded enthusiastically. "Did you know that one in ten people don't have access to clean water?"

And then she was off, discussing the intricacies of the issue, passionately advocating for why this was a cause close to her heart, and describing all the ways she was working to make clean water a reality for every person.

I pulled into the restaurant parking lot, finding a vacant spot near the entrance.

"Sorry," Laura finally said with a self-conscious laugh I immediately detested. "I get carried away when I talk about something I'm passionate about."

I unclipped my seat belt and reached across to wrap my hand around the back of her neck and gently squeeze. "Queenie, don't ever apologize for something you're enthusiastic about. You obviously love what you do, and you're passionate about this charity. The fact you can do both is exciting." I squeezed again. "Let's go celebrate. You can tell me more over dinner. I'm proud of you."

She blinked twice, a grin bursting across her pretty face, lighting her up.

"Sounds great."

The restaurant was a family-run bistro down towards the main pier in town. I'd been going there since I was young enough to remember. The food was seasonal and always delicious, the service warm and genuine.

And the view? Well, it had gotten me laid more than once.

Laura's intake of breath as we entered and upon seeing the beauty of the water stretched out for miles before us, had my cock twitching.

We're gonna get lucky tonight.

I mentally slapped myself.

Laura was dressed in a flattering black dress and wedge heels. Her hair was up in a little bun thing that had stray hairs dancing down her cheeks and neck. She looked soft and inviting. Until you looked at her chest, and then she was pure siren.

The neck of the dress had little crisscross straps above the curve of her breasts, in addition to a deep v that emphasized her abundance.

Every time I looked at her, I wanted to lick the curves of her breasts. I wanted to free them and suck her nipples, I wanted to fuck her against a wall while her tits bounced free in time to the thrusting of my cock.

I'd had a hard-on since before we'd left the house, and no amount of thinking about things like taxes and baseball stats was budging it.

We were seated at a table close to the windows, Laura sighing happily as she propped her face on her palm and gazed out.

"You really love the water," I remarked, enjoying watching her across the table.

"It's always been my dream to live close to it. I love the smell and the sounds and just... everything, you know?"

I chuckled. "Yeah."

She sighed, pushing back and opening the menu. "Wow, this looks fantastic."

"You really can't go wrong with anything here."

We settled on a chef's sampler, six courses with three samples of dessert. The night stretched on, us sharing and remarking on the food, Laura sharing about her life, and me sharing mine.

This woman is incredible.

I couldn't shake my attraction to her. Fact was, she was amazing, and the more I spoke to her, the more I wanted her in my life, my kid's lives, and my bed.

You're a lost cause.

Yep, and I didn't regret it for one moment. I suddenly understood how my brother could decide to move across the country, shack up with a woman, and decide to get married in less than six months.

I'd known Laura less than two weeks, and I already wanted her to be the mother of my kids and any future kids we had.

Crazy? Probably.

Taking on not only me but two kids would be asking a lot of anyone. But Laura didn't seem phased by the masters of mess.

The bill arrived, and I was more than ready to take this home. We'd been flirting outrageously all night, the awareness building between us as our fingers lingered, our eyes met and held, the smiles and innuendo becoming just that fraction more knowing.

"Home?" I asked quietly.

"Sounds perfect," Laura replied, rising from the table.

We exited the restaurant, and Laura tucked under my arm, one of her arms wrapped around my middle, the other pressed to my stomach, our bodies brushing as we moved, laughing and chatting on the way out to the car.

"Erik?" A familiar voice threw an icy bucket of water over my mood.

I froze, Laura stiffening as she registered my reaction.

I turned us slowly, reluctantly, seeing Claire and her husband standing by their car. She smiled, looking over at Laura and then back to me.

"Erik, I thought that was you." She stepped away from her car, coming towards us, her arms out as if she were about to hug me. "It's so great to run into you."

Laura disengaged, allowing Claire to wrap her arms around me. I remained frozen, like a stone, my emotions in lockdown as she squeezed.

She still wears Chanel.

Her perfume clung to me, overwhelming my senses.

She stepped back, smiling brightly at Laura. "Hi, I'm Claire. I'm sure Erik has told you all about me."

Laura took her hand, a fake smile pasted on her face. "Yes, of course," she lied.

"We're in town for Connor's sister's wedding." Claire grinned at her husband. "Thought we'd take advantage of staying with family and get a night out and away from the baby."

They have a baby.

She looked back at me, her smile still on her face. "It's so lovely to see you, Erik. Have a good night."

She turned, walking back to her car and sliding in. Laura slipped an arm back around my waist, and we watched silently as they pulled out and drove away.

"She's the one who broke your heart?" Laura asked quietly.

My chest deconstructed, the air suddenly rushing out as the ice in my veins melted at her straightforwardness. "Yeah."

"Seems like a bitch."

A startled laugh burst from my lips. "What?"

Laura shrugged. "Introduced herself but doesn't ask about me. Talks about herself, drops how happy they are with the baby thing, and then leaves. Doesn't once ask how you are or what our relationship is."

"Well... fuck," I muttered. "You got her number."

Laura gestured at the pier. "Wanna talk about it?"

I looked down at the beautiful woman beside me. "Actually, yeah."

"Let me get my coat from the car, and we can go for a walk."

"Okay."

CHAPTER 8

Laura

I snuggled into my coat as we walked the length of the pier. It was a beautiful spring night, if not a little chilly. But the moon was high, the breeze soft, and the stars bright. The waves crashed comfortingly as we strolled. At the pier, there was a set of stairs which took you down to the beach.

I led, kicking off my shoes at the bottom and sighing in pleasure as the sand wedged between my toes.

We strolled in companionable silence, sitting down under the pier, sheltered from the breeze and curious eyes.

"It's not a long story," Erik finally said, his

hip and leg pressed against mine as we settled in the sand. "Just a sucky one."

I glided fingers through the sand, head tilted his way, listening.

"We'd been together for three years. I'd thought she was the one. She'd refused to move into the little apartment I owned above the shop and said she had no room for me in her one bedroom. So, I'd been looking for a new place. An agent had just finished showing me a two-bedroom condo when she'd walked out of the apartment across from the open for inspection. I got to see her make out with him while I just stood there. That was a fun experience."

He looked at me, a wry smile on his lips. "Then she married him."

"Damn," I muttered, pulling my legs up to my chin and resting my head on them. "That is sucky."

"We broke up, obviously. But it fucked me up, you know? She said she hadn't seen a future with me, but she hadn't known how to break up with me either."

"I'm sorry," I reached out a hand, giving him a squeeze.

He lifted one shoulder. "You know, seeing her tonight, it was actually kind of cathartic, if you can believe it."

"Mm?"

Erik looked at the ocean for a long moment then turned to me. "Makes me realize we were never meant to be. I always thought I'd feel something if I ran into her. Like anger or regret maybe? Tonight, I was shocked, sure. But now I've seen her, and I've processed, honestly, I feel nothing but relief. It was shitty what she did, sure. But maybe it was right."

"Right?" I asked softly, not following.

"Mm, we weren't meant to be. But you and I?" He raised my hand pressing a kiss to my knuckles. "Tell me there's something here. Tell me I'm not the only one feeling this."

I stared into his dark eyes, seeing the hunger and hope, knowing mine reflected the same.

I opened my mouth to deny it but the words eluded me. "There's something," I admitted. "It's a hell of a big something."

"But?"

I swallowed, laying myself bare. "But I want this career I've started. I want to travel and help people. I want to be Laura Sweep, the Queen of Clean. I want to make a difference."

"And you think you can't if we take this further?"

"I don't know. You have kids. How would you feel about me travelling so much?"

"Babe." Erik leaned in, his face serious. "I'd never ask you to give up your career or who you are. You can't love someone for who you want them to be. You love someone for who they are. You're Laura, Queen of Clean. You're genuine and open, and if you have to travel to do that, then fine. We'll make it work. That's what people do."

That's what people do.

Was it really this simple? Was it really as easy as saying yes to him?

We haven't even slept together yet.

My body and heart said it would be amazing, but my brain was crying out for some rational thought. There was no logic in how we were feeling, no explanation for how rapidly this relationship was progressing.

Do it. Take a leap of faith.

"Okay," I whispered, then repeated it louder and with more conviction. "Okay. Let's do this. Let's work out what this is between us, let's explore it and build it and... and...." I paused, overwhelmed. "Let's be us."

Erik surged to his feet, hauling me up with him. "Come on," he ordered, pulling me along. I laughed, the wind clutching at my hair as we sprinted through the sand.

"Where are we going?" I asked, laughing at his determined expression.

"The workshop, it's closer than home, and there's a bed."

We hurried over the sand, stopping to kiss and touch, laughing as we tumbled and fumbled our way along the beach towards the marina.

Erik pulled a key from his pocket, opening the door at the back of a large warehouse. I pressed against him, biting playfully at his shoulder as he pushed it open. He laughed, pulling me inside and kicking the door shut. His body pressed to mine, warm, hard and smelling of salt, sand and man.

I tasted laughter and need on his lips, opening to let him taste me in return.

We stripped in the doorway and on the stairs leading up to the apartment. A trail of clothing marked our path.

Perhaps I should have felt self-conscious or anxious, especially as I'd just seen Erik's ex, and she was beautiful.

But I didn't. I felt nothing but desire. Desire for this man, desire for connection, desire for the things we were doing and about to do. In large part, that was thanks to Erik. He murmured deliciously filthy requests as he stripped my clothes from my body. His touch reverent but commanding. He kissed me and looked at me and touched me like I was the only thing in his universe that he wanted.

He lay me on the bed, immediately pulling at the last of my clothes. He discarded my underwear and dropped to his knees.

"Been dreaming of this." He leaned in, hovering for one protracted second, anticipation spiking before he closed his mouth over my pussy.

"Yes," I breathed, eyes closing, hands gripping the headboard above me. "God, yes."

Erik licked me with an attention I couldn't help but commend. His talented tongue and lips set my hips wiggling. I groaned encouragement as he worshipped me.

If I were the sacrifice and he the priest, this was an altar on which I would gladly die.

I came in a crescendo of feeling. Every cell in my body exploded with the joy and crazy emotion that came with a satisfying orgasm delivered by someone you love.

Love?!

I didn't have time to get stuck on that. Erik commanded all my attention as he surged up the bed. Gloriously naked, I had only a moment to appreciate three things – he was beautifully made, gorgeously proportioned, and he had a huge dick.

Yay me!

My body lit up as he pressed down, his mouth falling to my breasts. He kissed them, pulling first one nipple, then the other into his mouth. He laved them with attention, and stroked them, his mouth branding my body, wrecking me one tantalizing touch at a time.

"My turn," I finally told him, flipping us over. I sat up, legs straddling him as I ran fingers down his delectable chest.

Erik grinned up at me, tucking one hand behind his head, his bicep flexing in the most wonderful way. A chunk of hair fell over his forehead, while under me, his body relaxed.

"Your wish is my command."

Mm, yes it is.

It was my turn to drive him mad. I tasted my way down his body. With agonizing slowness, I revealed his secrets. Erik had sensitive nipples. There was a spot by his hip that made goose-pimples break out across his skin. He had a tattoo over his heart with the names of his boys hidden within.

I loved on his body, enjoying his uneven breathing, loving the grunts and groans as I explored. As I moved lower, those groans changed to whispered orders. And like any good girl, I completely ignored him.

I lowered my mouth to Erik's cock, positioning myself just so. I looked at him, his eyes darkly intense as he glowered at me hungrily.

"Ready?" I asked, purposefully breathy, knowing the heat of my mouth would heighten his anticipation.

"God help me if you don't—"

I swallowed him, his cock hitting the back of my throat as he broke off with a strangled curse.

"Fuck, Queenie. Laura, suck me. More!" The orders flew thick and fast, and I found that, unlike before, now I was powerless to ignore him. I needed to please, needed to give him what he wanted.

I swallowed his cock, my tongue teasing the head, my mouth hot and needy as I tasted, teased and choked on his length.

A dark part of me liked that.

My body hummed with need, my thighs slick with wet when Erik finally broke. His hands hooked under my arms and hauled me up his body. He took a bare second to position me, his gaze meeting mine as he thrust up and in.

A scream ripped from my throat, his cock filling me in the most perfect of ways.

"Fuck," he grunted, thrusting again. "Tight, hot, perfect."

He pinned me in place above him, my tits bouncing as his cock plundered my body. One hand dropped, his thumb finding my clit.

He circled once, twice, and then I broke. Body arching, hair tumbling, my pussy milked his cock as I came, his name tearing from my lips. Erik followed a moment later, groaning as he emptied inside me.

I collapsed on his chest, and his arms immediately held me tight as we breathed through the aftermath.

"Erik?"

"Mm?"

"I think you broke me."

He chuckled, his body moving mine. "Ditto."

We fell silent. His hands trailed soft strokes up and down my back.

"This is real, isn't it?" I looked up, finding his eyes at half-mast, a satisfied smile on his face.

"Oh, yeah." He pressed a kiss to my forehead, his arms tightening around me. "You got a problem with that?"

"No," I admitted, unable to conjure a single protest. "But that could be the sex talking."

He chuckled again, rolling us, so he loomed over me. "Then I better keep you sexually satisfied."

He lowered his head to kiss me again, and I had to admit, the man certainly knew how to satisfy.

CHAPTER 9

Laura

I'd woken Erik up with a blow job, he'd reciprocated by licking me until I came. Twice.

A girl could get used to this.

We'd spent the rest of Sunday hanging out with his sons, making out while they napped, and generally relaxing and getting to know each other. When we'd picked them up, Rune had silently handed me three books. Two were parenting guides geared towards step-parents, the last a novel I'd been wanting to read but hadn't had time to pick up.

Erik had explained this was Rune's way of showing approval. His super power was knowing the exact book you wanted, and he showed approval by giving it to you.

He'd never gifted a book to Erik's ex, and I couldn't help but feel slightly smug about that.

Monday dawned far too early, with the crew arriving for the final week of filming.

It took less than ten minutes for Liv to realize the dynamic between Erik and I had changed. She pulled me aside, crossing her arms over her chest, her eyebrows raised in question.

"What?" I asked, trying not to grin.

"Don't what me, missy. Spill."

I zipped my smiling lips, pretending to throw away the key.

"Hussy," Liv rolled her eyes, zero heat in her words. "Fine, just promise me you'll be gentle with him."

"I promise."

She sighed. "Guess it was too good to be true. Are you going to at least see this season out?"

I tilted my head to one side. "Liv, why would you think I'd be quitting?"

She blinked. "You're not?"

"No," I scoffed. "And Erik would kill me if I did. We talked about it. We're gonna make it work. It'll mean that we'll have to restructure the show. I don't want to do more than two weeks away from the boys at a time, but I think we could make it work."

Liv blinked at me rapidly. "Laura."

"Mm?"

"My brother is an idiot if he doesn't marry you."

I laughed; tension I hadn't realized I was carrying easing from my shoulders.

——

The rest of the week was a flurry of activity as we wrapped up filming. In between takes, Erik had done his best to manage his business, meet our filming requirements, and juggle his daddy responsibilities.

I found myself falling more in love with the man who seemed bound and determined not to let anyone down.

Love.

That was a word that hadn't passed through either of our lips yet. But it hovered on the tip of my tongue like a secret waiting to be shared.

Maybe today.

I'd woken up early, finding the house strangely quiet. Yesterday had been our final day of filming. After I'd returned home to pack up my life, I'd be returning in a few weeks for the recap and to move in with Erik.

A terrifying thought.

I couldn't wait.

I'd slipped out of the bedroom, leaving Erik passed out on the bed. He'd immediately shifted, pulling my pillow into him and burrowing deep. The man was a shameless snuggler.

I took a cup of coffee out to the jetty, dangling my feet over the side of the dock, sipping coffee as I watched the rising sun twinkle across the water.

"Last day today," Erik remarked, settling down beside me some time later. He handed me a fresh cup of coffee; a donut balanced on the lid.

I grinned, taking a bite.

He placed his own cup and donut beside him, pulling the baby monitor from his sweat pants pocket and setting it down behind us.

We sat in companionable silence, enjoying the morning light.

"Once upon a time," Erik said. "I dreamed of something like this. Kids in bed, sleeping peacefully. Sharing an early morning with my woman." He glanced at me, his heart stopping grin in place. "This is better than any dream."

I sighed, relaxing into him. "I didn't see you coming, Erik Larsson."

"Is that a bad thing?"

I chuckled. "No, definitely not."

"I love you, Laura."

The words registered and my heart expanded, warmth washing over me as his declaration settled in my soul.

"I love you, too."

We sealed our declaration with a kiss then pressed our heads together, grinning.

Applause interrupted our moment. Heads still pressed together, we turned, finding Erik's family – his *entire* family – as well as the crew watching us.

Correction, filming us.

Erik sighed. "Sure you want to join this madhouse? There's still time to bail out."

With all the love in my heart, I gave him my final answer. "Nope, you're stuck with me now."

"Thank fuc—um, fudge." And with that Erik kissed me.

EPILOGUE ONE

Laura

Three months later

"It's live!" Liv yelled from the lounge. Her announcement was followed by a stampede as all the Larsson's ran to get in place.

I exchanged a glance with Ella, Erik's soon-to-be-sister-in-law. She rolled her eyes, letting out a little laugh.

"Welcome to the family." She picked up a massive bowl of popcorn. "Get used to the stampede of marauders. It doesn't get any less loud."

I grabbed two giant packets of chips and followed her into the lounge. Gunnar, seated in the armchair, had grabbed his fiancé and was lifting her onto his lap, pressing kisses to her neck as she giggled and wiggled, trying to keep the popcorn upright.

I looked at Erik, finding him grinning at his brother.

"You wanna keep the PDA to a minimum?" He asked, reaching over and removing the bowl from Ella's hands.

"Nah, I'm good," Gunnar replied, immediately taking advantage of Ella's free hands to pull her into him and kiss her.

I laughed, tossing the chips on the table and making a leap for Erik. "Come on, I think we can take them in the obnoxiously adorable couple stakes."

He pulled me in, murmuring, "I'm up to the challenge."

I peppered his face with kisses, then squealed when he fell onto the couch, pulling me down and across him.

"Boys!" Jemma, Erik's mother, snapped. "Leave the girls alone. I want to watch this before the children wake."

I laughed, rolling off Erik and settling in beside him. He draped an arm around my shoulders, immediately pulling me into him. Ella made a move but Gunnar kept her tight against him keeping her on his lap.

It's almost like they're related.

I hid my amused smile, waiting for Liv, Astrid, and Rune to find their seats. Sune, Erik's dad, handed me a beer.

"You ready for this?" He asked, settling beside me on the couch.

"Definitely."

"I'm not," Erik grumbled. "You sure we have to do this?"

"Yes!" came the resounding answer from around the room.

I chuckled, patting Erik's leg. "Sorry, Babe. Looks like you're outnumbered."

He sighed heavily, "fine. Get on with it, then."

Sune hit play, and the episode started.

"Oh, Erik," Jemma whispered when they showed the mold in his bathroom. "Really?"

"Sorry, Ma. It's gone now."

She shook her head, shoving a mouthful of popcorn in her mouth.

Sune leaned over. "She's been singing your praises to the extended family."

"She has nothing to thank me for," I replied as the footage moved to our cleaning Erik's kitchen. "He did all the hard work."

The episode continued with his family ribbing him when they showed the storage container footage and sorting through his mess.

It showed me educating him on stain removal for the boys, and discussing the fifteen-minute-a-night rule for cleaning – the one I used so I didn't let mess pile up and waste my weekend.

The footage rolled, showing the final day of filming before I left. It was me talking about my experience and what I hoped for Erik and his twins.

"I hope that he finds a little piece of peace in what I've taught him. It's not easy being a single parent, and I have nothing but love and admiration for him."

The final footage showed me hanging the St Johanna jersey I'd had framed in his office before leaving.

"Why don't you do something like that for me?" Sune asked Jemma.

"Because you support the Hogs," she returned, not even offering him a glance.

I sniggered.

"Is that it?" Astrid asked as the screen went dark. She leaned forward, snatching the final handful of popcorn from the bowl.

"No, there's the recap where Laura returns a few weeks later for a visit." Liv rubbed her hands together. "It's always the part where people cry."

I glanced at Erik, raising an eyebrow in question. He shook his head, rolling his eyes.

"Don't get your hopes up."

I laughed, snuggling into his side.

The footage began, and I frowned, glancing up at Erik. "This isn't the recap."

"Isn't it?" he asked, giving me a surprised look. "It's what I remember filming."

"Hey, I'm Erik," said the image of Erik on the TV. "And I'm a recovering mess-a-holic."

I laughed delighted.

"Thanks for watching this episode where the Queen of Clean comes in and bails out my dorky daddy butt. Laura, you've changed my life. Completely."

The footage cut to a montage of him and his boys with... me. The images and video were taken from the weeks we'd cleaned his house and ended with the image of Erik and I kissing that morning on his deck, the morning sun behind us.

"Erik," I whispered, looking up. "We look like we're in a love story?"

"That's because we are." He grinned nodding at the screen. "Keep watching, Queenie."

"Just to be perfectly transparent, Laura's moved herself in." Screen Erik said. "And thank god for that because I love her."

The screen cut to a phone video recorded

by Liv. We were holding the boys, laughing over hamburgers.

"Are you sure you want to move in with this guy?" Liv asked from behind the camera.

I'd juggled Ulf on my lap, laughing as I tossed a chip at Erik. "O'm up for the challenge."

It cut back to Erik.

"Laura, you may have cleaned out my house, but you've filled my heart." Screen Erik got down on one knee. "Will you marry me?"

I glanced up, finding Erik watching me. "Are you serious?"

"Completely." He pulled a ring out of the gap between the sofa seat cushion and arm, holding it up. "Laura Sweep, Queen of Clean, my Queenie. Will you marry me?"

I may have stuttered the word. Or maybe I shouted it. Or maybe I didn't say anything. I couldn't remember. Just like the day we'd first met, my mind went blank, and all I could see, taste, smell, and feel was him.

Erik. *My* Erik.

He slid the ring on my finger as he kissed me, tasting just as wonderful today as the first time we'd kissed. Tears of joy ran down my cheeks as his family squealed and leapt about, showering us with congratulations and slowly pulling us apart.

Someone retrieved the twins, and they were passed around, making their way to Erik and me as his mother squished us together for a photo.

I held Leif, Erik holding Ulf as we gazed at each other, happiness in our every line.

"You're stuck with us now," he told me, pulling me close to press a kiss to my forehead.

"Guess you better get used to a clean house then."

"Queenie, nothing turns me on more than watching you clean my pipes."

"Overshare!" Gunnar yelled, making a face. "Jesus, brother!"

We laughed as his mother took the picture. It was the image I'd use on social media to announce our engagement. The image that the papers would publish and the fans would gush over.

And it was the image that would hang in our bedroom beside our wedding photo.

It was the image of pure joy.

EPILOGUE TWO

Erik

Three years later

"Want Momma!" Leif yelled, stamping his little foot in protest. "Buddy, I've already told you, Momma's on an airplane, remember?"

"Swoosh!" Ulf said from beside me, his arms shooting straight out as he swayed from side to side.

"Got it in one, Bud," I praised. I lifted the shirt once more, prepared to bargain with my stubborn son.

"Come on, Leif. If you put your shirt on, I'll let you have some chocolate milk with breakfast. Just don't tell your mom, deal?"

He considered the deal, eyeing the shirt with suspicion. "Ulf too?"

"Sure," I promised, desperate to seal the deal.

"O-tay." He thrust his arms up in the air, waiting for me to slip it on.

I sighed in relief, wrestling the shirt into place. Finally dressed, we then shared breakfast —the naughty chocolate milk treat, greedily devoured – then grabbed our pre-packed bags to head to Grandma's.

"Okay, boys," I yelled shoving them through the door at my mom. "Have fun!"

"Erik, you don't want to come in for a–"

"No time!" I yelled, frantic. "Gotta go, love you, Ma!"

I heard my dad laughing from inside as Ma stood in the doorway, a frown in place as she watched me practically sprint for my car.

Call me a terrible parent, but I'd lied to my kids. And I felt zero shame.

Momma wasn't still on an aeroplane. Momma's plane had already landed, and she was in a cab on her way home right now.

And she had been sexting Daddy for over three days. The woman was about to be punished.

I, barely, managed to stay within the speed limit as I drove home, managing to pull into the driveway just as the cab pulled up to the curb.

I parked, threw open the door and slammed it shut, clicking the lock as I headed for my woman.

She stepped from the cab, her handbag over one shoulder, looking daisy fresh and entirely fuckable in a beautiful summer dress that hugged every curve.

"Hey stranger," she called, a smile lighting her face.

God, she's stunning.

I thought it every time I saw her. Thought it every time she returned from her trips. I'd thought it the day she'd walked down the aisle to me, flowers in her hair, that gorgeous smile on her lips.

I stalked to her, pulled her close, my lips meeting hers in a hungry kiss.

"Damn honeymooners," the driver muttered, getting out and unloading Laura's bags.

I ignored him, focusing on my wife.

It'd been three years since Laura had entered my mess of a house and set everything to right. She'd made this house a home, loved on my boys, loved on me.

She still had her career, her show winning an Emmy last year. Her social media numbers were through the roof and only increasing, with endorsement deals coming her way every day. We made it work because it was worth it. Every single moment we had together made all the stress and juggling, and travel worth it.

"Missed you," she murmured against my lips.

"Missed you more," I replied.

We backed up just a little, Laura still in my arms but trying to peer around me.

"Where are my boys?" she asked, frowning.

"Grandmas."

Laura looked up at me, a sexy grin pulling at her lips. "Oh really?"

"Mm." I bent to kiss her again but was interrupted by the driver.

"Sorry," he muttered. "You need anything else?"

"No, thanks."

We waved him off then I picked up her bags and followed her into the house.

"Erik," she said with a delighted laugh. "You didn't."

I dropped the bags in the entry, closing the door behind me and coming to wrap arms around her middle, resting my head on her shoulder. "It's the one you wanted, right?"

She looked at me, heart in her eyes. "Yeah, and it's perfect."

I'd long ago learned that the way to Laura's heart wasn't through flowers or chocolate – though she liked those as well. Nope, the best gift was a new cleaning instrument.

This time I'd gone big. To be fair, it was the longest she'd been away – three weeks in total. I'd missed her, the boys had missed her, our house missed her.

Don't tell her, but I'd had the family come over yesterday to help tidy. She may be the Queen of Clean, but I was certainly still the Master of Mess. And the last thing I'd wanted today was something to distract her.

She pulled away, running hands over the industrial-grade carpet cleaner.

"It's gorgeous," she murmured, lifting the hose. "Ooh, lightweight and ergonomic."

Honestly. My wife was the only woman I knew who would want a vacuum more than diamonds. Seriously, the woman had a Pinterest dream board filled with what she called 'cleaning porn'.

That's my wife.

"You can admire it later." I swung her up and over my shoulder, and headed for the stairs.

She squealed, her legs kicking in my fireman hold. "Erik! Put me down! You'll do your back!"

I ignored her, zeroing in on our bedroom.

Three weeks of no sex. Three weeks of not seeing her, smelling her, tasting her.

Too fucking long.

I deposited her on the bed, covering her with my body, my lips finding hers.

We came together, a desperate, dirty mess of grasping limbs, gasping breath and glorious release.

After, we lay together, side-by-side, on the bed. Both of us panting as we came down off a fucking incredible high.

"Never doing three weeks again," Laura muttered, her eyes closed.

"Thank fudge for that."

She chuckled, eyes still closed. "I brought you a present."

I perked up, finding energy I thought she'd drained. "Present?"

She chuckled, rolling to her side. "It's in my purse."

I went downstairs, found her discarded purse and carried it back to the room. When she said purse, she really meant giant-fucking-handbag. Honestly, it was like Mary Poppins had handed over her magic tricks. We'd once blown two tires and spent over four hours on the side of the road waiting for AAA. The woman had produced food, clean wipes and a miraculous amount of entertainment for our sons from the depths of that thing.

I handed it over. "Is it sexy?" I asked, hopefully.

"Not quite." She tugged a small wrapped gift free, handing it over.

I shook it, listening. "It doesn't jingle. Or bark."

"Nope," she said, smiling.

"Hmm, so it's not a pony?"

"Sadly, no."

"Damn." I ran a finger along the edge of the wrapping paper, ripping it clean through. She watched, biting her lip as I pulled the cloth free. I shook it out, blinking as I registered the tiny onesie. A onesie that read; *My Daddy owns Thor's Shipbuilding*.

I looked from the onesie, down to Laura, back to the onesie, then back to Laura.

"Queenie, does this mean...?"

She nodded, a grin bursting across her face. "Turns out I didn't have the stomach flu while in Grand Harbour."

I fisted the onesie in one hand as I pulled her to me with my other. "Are you okay? How do you feel? Shit, do we need to schedule a doctor? How far along are you?"

She laughed, holding me close.

"Erik, it's gonna be fine. We're only about

eight weeks along. I've scheduled a doctor's appointment for tomorrow. I've had a little nausea in the mornings, but nothing crazy."

I bent, pressing a kiss to her mouth. "Queenie, I don't know what to say."

"Are you happy?"

"Fucking ecstatic," I pressed another kiss to her mouth, then another. Somehow more turned on by the knowledge I'd planted a baby in her. The blood of my ancestors sang through my veins, demanding I celebrate by branding this woman.

She. Is. Mine.

This time I paid closer attention to her body, noticing subtle changes. Her breasts were more sensitive. Her body more responsive.

I rolled her so she could ride me, watching her breasts bounce, her body move as she rode us to victorious release.

My Laura, my full-bodied, gloriously talented, wonderfully intelligent, amazing Laura was pregnant.

We both came again, me bellowing her name, Laura on a broken scream. She fell beside me, panting, and I couldn't stop myself from leaning down and pressing a kiss to her stomach.

She laughed, swatting at my head.

"Do you think it's a girl or a boy?" I asked, grazing my fingers across her stomach.

"I don't mind."

"The boys will be happy."

"Don't I know it. Do you think they'll let up on the puppy idea?"

"Not a chance."

We both laughed.

Laura yawned, rubbing one eye. "The only other downside is the fatigue."

"Stay here, have a nap. There's nothing you need to do. I'll deal with your luggage."

I sailed through the housework, unpacking her stuff, doing the laundry, and deciding to throw on a crockpot for dinner that night.

I went back up to the bedroom with a sandwich and a tall glass of water. I'd spent the last hour googling what pregnant women could and couldn't eat, and had already placed an order for home delivery.

Gotta nail this husband-of-a-pregnant wife role.

Laura was still passed out on the bed, gently snoring.

I took a moment just admiring this magnificent woman before I placed the plate and glass quietly on the bedside table.

Then I bent, pressing a soft kiss to her belly.

"Welcome to the family, little Viking."

Thank you for reading Clean Sweep!
Next up is The X-List featuring Rune and his
surprise love interest who just so happens to be a
non-reader!
THE WORST!

Desperate for more Laura and Erik?
Get a BONUS slice of life on EvieMitchell.com

ABOUT THE AUTHOR

Hey, I'm Evie Mitchell.
I'm a thirty-something romance author (she/her/hers) living with disability. I believe in inclusion, accessibility, and fierce romance. My loves include steamy romance novels, my sexy husband, our THREE sausage dogs (THE FUR!!!), and my ever-growing collection of book-related mugs.

As a woman with a diverse work history, including in areas such as hospitality, retail, emergency response, event management, human rights, disability access, and security— my books are filled with true stories (bridezillas), worst-case scenarios (malfunctioning zippers), and my favorite tropes (one-bed).

I'm a strong proponent of #OwnVoices, and specialize in fiercely inclusive happily ever afters.

EvieMitchell.com
Socials: @EvieMitchellAuthor

All Access Series

Knot My Type

Love Flushed

Darn Knit All

Larsson Siblings

Thunder Thighs

The X-List

Reality Check

The Christmas Contract

The A-List

Capricorn Cove

The Shake-up

Double the D

Muffin Top

The Mrs. Clause

New Year, Knew You

Double Breasted

As You Wish

You Sleigh Me

Meat Load

Resolution Revolution

Dogg Pack

Puppy Love

Bad English

The Frock Up

Pier Pressure

Trick or Trent

New Year's Faye

Reigning Hearts

The Marriage Claim

Silent Knight

Men of Trinity Bay

Kink in the Road

Nameless Souls MC

Runner

Wrath

Ghost

Shield

Elliot Security

Rough Edge
Bleeding Edge